I Hate Writing

Creative Writing for Reluctant Writers

Amanda J Harrington

Author of the Creative Writing for Kids series &

Creative Comprehensions

Contents

Introduction

I Hate Writing Stories! is written for parents who really want to help their child with **literacy** but are unsure where to start or what to do for the best. Funny, helpful and sympathetic, the focus is always on helping children to understand **creative writing** and use literacy in new ways.

Each chapter covers a different type of approach, building through the book so that children can write stories independently and without stress. All the exercises have full **example answers**, to help both parents and children.

The exercises are **flexible** and can be used for different ages and abilities. There is **advice** throughout on how to adapt the work to suit children who find writing itself difficult.

All the work can be repeated using new ideas, so that the book can continue to help children with their literacy long after it has first been completed. **Extra exercises** and ideas are given at each stage, as well as **optional work** for children who are ready.

In-depth explanations are given in most chapters, to help parents understand how each exercise is useful and to explain why children find some things so difficult in literacy.

Amanda J Harrington is a professional tutor and home educator, with years of experience helping children of all ages and abilities achieve their potential in literacy. The exercises in this book have been used in real educational situations, as well as informally with children at home.

I Hate Writing Stories! is part of the Creative Writing for Reluctant Writers series and can be paired with A Month of Stories, also available on Amazon and other reputable online sources.

Story Talk

Think of a place you have been

This exercise is an activity where you can help your child find ways to describe places, events, experiences and join in yourself. There is no writing involved, unless you have a go at the optional exercise near the end. For now, we are just freeing up some ideas and helping your child to find different ways to be creative.

Story Talk is split into sections which can be done at different times. Read through the whole of this chapter before you start, so that you don't have to interrupt your child once they start talking and remembering.

For your practice exercise, you are going to think of a place you have both been. There are other ideas at the end of the chapter and you can make up your own once you are used to how it is done.

Talk

Discuss a place you have both been and what you did there. How many things can you remember? What did you see and hear? How many details can you think of as you talk about it together? What could you see and smell, touch and feel? What did you find or discover?

How many ways can you describe the place just by talking about it? How many different words can you use?

Don't be worried by the number of questions I am asking, all these are just to give you a push in the right direction. Once you start talking, you shouldn't need the help as you both start to remember.

Discuss it like a conversation *with a purpose*. You don't want to worry your child by making it seem too educational, but they should be aware it's going to become some kind of story. If there is anxiety about writing then be sure to make it clear there will be no writing this time, so they can relax and enjoy the activity.

Example conversation

Have a look at how you might set things off, bringing out details in a normal conversation.

Dad: Can you remember when we went to the fair last Summer? What do you think was the best part?

Alice: I liked going in the playhouse because you came with me and you were scared! You kept shouting every time something happened and I had to show you the way out.

Dad: I think I liked the big wheel the best, but it was a bit creaky.

Alice: We could see our house from the big wheel but it was slow and you shouted when it creaked.

Dad: I didn't shout! I liked the big wheel.

Alice: I think I'm braver than you are at fairs.

Do you see how a normal conversation can kick-start memories, as well as showing how two people remember things differently?

Summary

Once you have talked about it, summarise the main things you came up with. These could be along the lines of:

Where was it? What did you do? Who was there? What did you like? Main memories.

This summary can either be talked about or written down. If you want to write it down, then don't worry about writing it yourself. Knowing they don't have to write anything is part of the fun for your child, at this stage.

If you do write it down for them, then be sure to include everything they have thought of, so they feel part of the process. If your child is happy, let them write the sentences themselves. It can be a fluid, flexible activity, simply be guided by what is best for you both.

Example summary

Here is the summary of our conversation above. Notice how it starts to look more like a story once you write it all down, especially if you put yourselves as characters, rather than describing it as 'we went' etc.

Dad and Alice went to the fair and tried nearly all the rides. Dad didn't like the playhouse because it was too small inside and he kept getting stuck. Alice had to show him where to get out. Then they tried to win a bear at the stall but spent too much money and still didn't get a bear.

The big wheel was really big and creaky and Dad worried about the noises it made when they went round. Alice could see their house from the top, even the blue bit that was the trampoline in the front garden.

At the end, Dad and Alice had some chips on the way home and decided they would come back next year.

The next stage

This part can take as long as you like, depending on whether your child is beginning to see it as too much like work! At this stage, you don't want to push the work side too much. Later exercises should be done all at once, but for now you can afford to be more relaxed and let your child get used to doing creative work.

What we want to avoid is making any negative feelings about creative writing even stronger. These early exercises are designed to show it's not all about writing the hated stories. Once your child realises it's not like being at school, they should relax and feel more confident, even if there is still complaining!

Draw

Now draw some pictures to show your main points. You can add extra details but try to steer the pictures around your summary above, so that they are clear and direct.

Don't worry about the quality of the drawing, the pictures are just a tool to help your child visualise what you have been talking about. And it isn't against the rules to use some words: you can label the pictures or even have a short sentence under each one, explaining what is happening.

Example picture

For Dad and Alice you would have a picture of the fair, which could either be one nice big one, showing all the rides, or separate pictures showing Dad stuck in the playhouse and Dad and Alice on top of the big wheel.

Can you imagine how the conversation and the summary might look in pictures? If you had a picture for all your main points, would it look a bit like a comic strip? For Dad and Alice, you might have the playhouse, then the win-the-bear stand, the big wheel, with their house in the distance and them walking home at the end, eating chips.

If you had one main picture, then the different places at the fun fair might be labelled, so you could have the playhouse with a label saying, 'this is where Dad got stuck' and so on.

Once you have done the pictures, your child might want to write more about what happened. Let them, without making it too important. Be relaxed about it, try not to look too eager while still giving encouragement.

Once you're happy with your pictures, have a little round-up discussion where you talk about how the pictures reflect what happened on the day. This reinforces the ideas you had and makes it easier to keep the images clear in your mind.

Gathering together

Using only what is in the house, let your child collect objects and things which can be linked to what you have discussed or drawn in the pictures. For example, if you talked about a holiday, you may have souvenirs, or clothes you wore while you were there, or even a bottle of suntan lotion!

The objects don't have to be directly linked to the place you talked about. If you talked about going somewhere on a very sunny day, you could find something yellow to represent the sun.

Try to gather a few things together, no less than 3 but no more than about 7 - you don't want it to become too confusing.

Example objects

For their trip to the fair, Dad and Alice find things which remind them of the visit. Alice has a tambourine to be the big wheel and Dad pretends the hamster cage is the funhouse.

They bring a few of Alice's bears to be on the win-the-bear stand and set them up on the edge of the sofa, so they can try knocking them off with a tennis ball.

Alice spends a happy time drawing and cutting out strips of paper, coloured in yellow, to be the chips.

While you're gathering, or once you have everything together, talk about how the objects relate to your discussion and the pictures. Can you link up pictures with objects, like a matching game?

Don't underestimate the simple matching process. If your child struggles with creative writing, one of the things they probably find most difficult is thinking of ideas to write down. By showing them how real-life objects can be matched with memories and your conversations, you are helping your child use new ways of thinking to create ideas. This shows them there are lots of ways to come up with story ideas and many of them start with what you already know.

A Story!

This is an important moment. You have talked, shared memories, worked things out together. You have drawn pictures and gathered objects and helped each other to remember something. You have shared an experience.

This is the moment when you can tell your child that, together, you have created s story. The talking, pictures and real-life objects have all created a story without any words having to be written. Any words written down are a bonus.

It is very important for your child to come away with the understanding that stories do not have to be written to be real things which show truth and meaning. **Stories happen all around us, every day, they do not only exist inside books or at the end of a pen**.

Together you have created the story of a special place and made it into something new.

This exercise can be repeated using different ideas listed at the end of this chapter. With some practice, your child can complete this activity by themselves, but a lot of the fun is in doing it with someone else.

The discussion part needs to be done with another person anyway, but completing the whole activity with a partner is very rewarding. They can try with other family members or friends and see how differently it turns out.

Optional

And I mean optional! Do not fall into the trap of trying to make an activity become too educational, which can turn your child away from learning. This is a step-by-step process and you can always come back to this chapter later, when other stories have been written.

So, with that in mind, at the end of this activity, with enthusiasm still high, it might be possible to guide your child into writing about the place they remember.

Don't force this, they have created something without words, so they should only progress to words if they are truly ready or willing.

More Ideas

My best birthday

Playing in the snow?

My perfect pet

When I first went to school

Going to the beach

Playing in the garden

I did it by myself

The most exciting thing ever!

I hate stories because...

Okay, I admit it, this activity is a sneaky way to encourage writing. Bear with me though, as it is also a good way to talk about some of the things which really bother your child. It can help them to understand why they don't like doing some things and where their difficulties come from.

Reasons why

For this exercise, you are going to ask your child to think of some of the reasons they don't like writing stories, then to explain in more detail why they feel that way. This is all background work to help you bring your child forward in creative writing and literacy, but it is also practice in describing how they feel.

They can do this work in writing or by talking to you. If they have real problems explaining how they feel, then let them draw pictures of smiley (or grumpy!) faces and work from there. Always consider starting in a small way and building up as this is easier for children to cope with than feeling they have to do everything at once.

Example Reasons

Here are some ideas to start with. Use them or add your own, but you must let your child explain *why* they feel the way they do.

I don't like reading, so I don't like writing either.

I do like reading, but that's different.

I don't like reading made-up stories, I like real stuff.

I'll write when I feel like it.

I hate writing when I'm told to.

I want to write about something exciting/better/more interesting,

I'd rather watch TV or play games.

I'd rather be outside.

Maths is better.

Anything is better than writing stories.

It makes me feel sad to write stories.

Everyone else can write better stories than me.

I just don't like it!

To be honest, a lot of children would naturally choose the last one, even if one of the other reasons was closer to the truth. Children become used to being asked why they don't like doing things, when the adult has the ulterior motive of making them do the thing anyway.

They know if they give the real reason, it might be used against them or denied as a proper reason not to like writing. So they will usually avoid saying how they really feel or hedge around the issue.

How do they feel?

Let your child choose a reason and work with it, but to be sure they are gaining the most from this exercise, consider letting them choose more than one, as a way of helping them open up and get to the root of their dislike.

It's important to encourage your child to choose reasons that describe how they feel, then to expand it as much as they can This is not school, you are not asking them to write about it as a punishment - you only want a little more detail to be added to the starter sentence.

It's a good idea for your child to say more about how they feel, but at this stage they don't have to write it all down. It's more important to find out how they feel than make them express it in writing.

Example explanations

Here are some of the reasons again, expanded. Remember, these are just suggestions, your child can say anything they like about writing – it's personal to them.

Anything is better than writing stories.

I can't write stories and I haven't got any better at it, so I would rather do anything else as at least other things can be learned.

Everyone else can write better stories than me.

I have to sit in class and watch everybody writing when I can't think of anything.

I hate writing when I'm told to.

If I could write about good stuff that I like, I might write more stories but we always have to write what the teacher wants or what other people choose.

Use your own example to help your child understand

If your child doesn't understand what they need to do, choose something that you don't like, such as shopping, visiting Aunt Thelma or driving in busy traffic and make an example that shows them how to explain something in more detail.. For instance, you could say:

I don't like eating fruit.

This would be your starter sentence, which you can add more detail and expand to:

I don't like eating fruit because it always takes too long and I don't like the taste.

You see how the original sentence becomes a little longer and makes it clear why you don't like eating fruit?

You should give your child an example that has nothing to do with writing stories as this means they can't copy what you have written. They will be used to taking any shortcuts possible to avoid writing at school and for homework, so don't help them to do it at home! What you need to concentrate on throughout is encouraging them to do their own work, while always being there to offer support.

In more depth

Sometimes, this discussion can be the kick-start you need to really get to the bottom of your child's difficulty with writing and literacy. It might bring out issues you weren't aware of or surprises that help you to understand your child's point of view.

On a practical level, by talking about the reasons your child doesn't like writing, you are helping them open up about things which can be worked on later. If you discuss things now, you can come back to writing them down, even if you have to repeat back to your child what they have said.

What can be uncomfortable or difficult for you as a parent is resisting the temptation to jump in and say 'encouraging' things like 'Well, if you like reading, you'll definitely like writing, we just need to get you started'.

Basically, do avoid saying things which influence the way your child responds to this exercise. Feel free to ask helpful questions, such as 'Why do you feel that way?' and also avoid leading questions like 'Didn't you enjoy the book about pixies that Santa brought you?'

This is not the time to go on about what a beautiful notepad Aunt Thelma bought or how many special pens you have given them, to make writing seem more like fun. Also, don't point out that your child used to enjoy writing but then turned against it. This sort of reaction is quite common and it's important to find out why it might have happened. But it won't be solved in a few minutes of intensive, and probably desperate, questioning.

The main aim with this exercise is to get you and your child thinking and communicating. You will want them to examine their dislike of creative writing and you should also look at the way you react to that dislike. In the case of trying to help them enjoy and explore creative writing, it is almost guaranteed to fail if we pile on the pressure. Relax, step back and let them think about it for themselves.

A Story in Pictures

Now, don't get excited or upset. Your child will be writing stories by the end of this book and I'm not letting them have a chapter of rest where they can draw and la-la about doing nothing important. Right, with that out of the way...

This chapter is all about the story: the beginning, the middle and the end; the plot, the ability to create an interesting dialogue and fill it with exciting events. All of these will apply, though don't frighten your child by telling them this right now. The only thing missing will be the written words.

Story base

For this exercise, your child should choose an event or a day that was full of interest and activity. Birthdays and Christmas are always a good choice, as are holidays or special days out. Something that was out of the ordinary is ideal.

Once the event has been chosen, your child can begin the creative part. Using pictures they have drawn themselves, cut out from magazines or found on the internet and printed off, your child should make a story about the event.

For instance, if they are thinking of a family holiday, you may be able to use actual pictures taken on that holiday, or images from the brochure or online advert for it.

Story stages

What needs to happen is that all stages of the story are described in pictures. So, staying with the theme of a holiday, what about the packing or the journey from home as a starting point? One picture could show everyone in a car, faces smiling through the windows. Or down at the beach, having fun and playing games.

Keep it simple, as the pictures need to tell the story without any words. You are aiming for someone who doesn't know the background to the activity being able to pick up your child's work and follow the main events as shown in the pictures.

Example story

If your child has chosen a birthday, then the stages could be something like this:

Rushing around, decorating the house for a party

Getting dressed for the party and putting the cake on a table

All the guests arrive

Party games

Opening presents

Cake and candles

A picture of your child, surrounded by friends and presents.

It can be better for the pictures to be hand drawn, so that extra, personal details can be inserted into the story, but don't push this. There are plenty of images online which can be used as inspiration to help the story along.

Guidance

Give some guidance to this activity. You need to explain that the story is very important, especially the order that things happened. It can be a good idea for each picture, whether drawn or printed or cut, to be done separately, so that they can be brought together, in the right order. There is always something that has been forgotten and keeping the pictures separate is a good way to avoid the upset of your child feeling the story is spoiled by them having left something out.

When the story is complete, look at it together and talk about what the different pictures represent. Try to overlook any small mistakes with the details or events; concentrate more on whether it is presented as a story with an order to it, showing that your child has considered the way it will look and 'read' to someone else.

In-depth

This is still early work and some of the activities used now are building foundations of greater confidence and willingness to try different things, even if those things are story-related. Always be ready with encouragement, while gently guiding your child to do work which links with instructions given in these chapters.

This activity can be re-done as many times as you like, with different events. With more confidence, it can also be used as a purely creative exercise, with your child making up every detail and basing their story on anything at all. The main reason for keeping it within reality at first is to give practice in ordering the events within the story, as it's easier to remember the order of events from real life than to work them out when making up an original story.

This exercise is also very good for renewing confidence later on. When your child is doing the more difficult chapters in this book, or having to complete school work which involves actual writing, it can be so useful to refer back to activities like this. Use them as a way of showing your child that they *can* create stories, from scratch, filled with their own ideas and hard work.

This exercise may be very different from the ones your child does in the future, but it is still creative and means thinking about stories in a proper, organised way. Don't ever let your child think they can't create stories, even if they are having real trouble with a current project. Each piece of work is different and every activity brings its own challenges. So, keep each activity or story your child completes and remind them of what they have achieved before, even if today's troubles seem too difficult.

Quick-fire and almost painless

I say *almost* painless because in this chapter we will be doing some writing. Not too much, not proper stories, so don't panic!

As an exercise in thinking on the spot, this chapter is designed to show your child they can come up with ideas for themselves, even if they don't turn those ideas into fully-fledged stories. All stories start with an idea and often if a child decides they hate creative writing, it is linked with the belief that they can't think of any ideas. The vicious circle completes when the pressure to think of ideas means none are forthcoming and without ideas there are no stories, so the child thinks they can't write stories.

You see how this goes round, preventing forward movement and perpetuating a feeling of failure and disappointment, which then turns into a stubborn determination not to like writing stories. Ever!

Thinking and writing

For now, we'll have a little bit of fast thinking, with no pressure to get it right or create more later. This is a simple set of quick idea-starters. If your child doesn't know anything about one of the subjects, miss it out. Pressure is being left outside, alone, in the hall today.

For each word or phrase, your child should think of as many things as they can which link with it. Time them for this, with a starting time of about 20 seconds. Make this time longer if you think your child needs it, or start with longer and shorten it as they try each word, so it becomes like a game.

Don't start with longer than a minute though, as it becomes too much like work if you make it too long and then stress creeps in.

Words

unicorn, stars, whales, bicycle, school, tea time, brushing, footsteps, wonder, fire light, petals, dancing, cold water, dog food, laughing, sneeze, kitchen, heat, banana, tremble, rhino, leaf

Thinking and doing

Now, using a similar method, we're going to expand the 20 second quick-thinking to another activity. Give your child another 20 seconds to search the house for objects which relate to words you make up yourself. These can be anything, but have the list ready before you start, so that everything is kept nice and quick (see further down for examples of this).

For instance, you might want to keep it simple and choose colours of the rainbow. Once your child has returned with a 'matching' item, such as a blue sock, for the colour blue, get them to write as many words as they can which link to the *object* they brought back, not the colour.

So, as you start with one idea, such as the colour, you then swap to a different idea, based on what was found. This is another way of making your child think on their feet, coming up with ideas in the safe environment of the home, in the form of a game.

Example thinking and doing

Starter idea of animals – child returns with a teddy, bunny slippers and a leopard-print top.

Teddy – bear, cuddly, soft, brown, bedtime

Bunny slippers – warm, black, cute, funny, a present

Leopard-print top – silky, yellow, black, summery, smooth

In-depth

This exercise helps your child to see what they can do when the pressure is off. It's always different at home, compared to school, but they have the same abilities in both places, if they are relaxed and confident enough to access them.

By creating activities at home which help your child to think of ideas for themselves, you are helping them to gain confidence so that they can do the same thing at school, where there is always more pressure.

The timing of this activity makes it more fun, as they have to think quickly. At school, time is also an issue and it is not usually fun! It becomes pressure instead. The trick is to help your child access information quickly, for fun, which will help them get used to picking out ideas with less hesitation, so helping them once they are at school.

Sometimes there is a lot more going on at school that is contributing to the problems your child has with writing. This can be bullying, or being generally unhappy in the classroom, or feeling left out. You can't solve all

32

these problems by practising creative writing at home, but by making one difficult area more manageable, you help your child to see that other difficulties can also be overcome.

Crazy Stories

Yes, there will be story writing in this chapter. Oh dear, shall we have a cup of tea first? No, let's get on with it, everything will be fine!

For this activity, you need some books with a good amount of writing in them. Picture books are fine as long as they have proper paragraphs with a few sentences in them. You want to choose books your child can read and understand without too much difficulty.

Closing their eyes, your child should open the book and let their finger fall on a word. Help guide their hand if necessary, so that they always find a word.

The word found should be written down on its own line, then the exercise repeated. Each time, give the word its own line and move on. Go through the books, choosing one word from each, then move onto the next book and back to the start.

Aim to have at least 10 words written down. If you get too many like 'and', 'if', 'too' and so on, more should be chosen. Also, if you do seem to be getting a lot like this, check your child is not cheating, as they will often choose joining words if they can because they see them as easier to work with.

You need to have a decent choice of describing words or naming words.

Example words

Your list might look something like this:

Packing

Young

Said

You

Come

Second

Gone

School

They

Fairy

Words into sentences

Now your child should write a sentence which includes one or more of the words. If your child is able to write a sentence with more than three of the words at a time, then limit them to using two at a time because their end story will be longer.

The sentences don't have to link to each other, they can be completely separate. This can make the story stranger but more entertaining for your story-hating child.

Example sentences

With my words I might make the following sentences: My original words are in bold so you can see how I expanded them out into full sentences.

*The **fairy school** is here.*

*The **young** cat had **gone**.*

*She **said** I was **second**.*

***They** finished **packing**.*

***You** can **come** too.*

Each sentence should make sense by itself but not yet be a story. Sometimes a story will happen by accident as your child develops the sentences, but mostly more work is needed.

Sentences into stories

Now, using **one** of those sentences, your child should try writing a very short story around it. The story can be no more than a sentence long if they like. Again, the emphasis is on it being less about pressure and more about letting the ideas out.

Example story

Here is my very short story:

'The fairy school is here,' I said to my friend. We searched in the bushes but only found twigs and leaves. The little school had gone and so had the fairies.

In-depth

It doesn't have to be a good story, an interesting one or even a proper one. It could read like the start of a story, or the end or even the middle. The aim is to use one of the sentences to create something new. Using words already existing in a book, your child can turn them into something unique to themselves.

A story, no matter how small or short, is an accomplishment. At school, it is most often necessary to write proper stories, long enough to be marked and judged. At home, stories can be anything we like and recognised as having value for lots of different reasons.

A child who hates creative writing will be very used to their work being thought of as not good enough or not long enough. By doing little exercises like this, they can see how stories and creative writing comes in lots of different shapes and sizes and be very personal to them.

A proper story!

Well, almost. Yes, it is a proper story, a really good one that has a beginning, a middle and an end. It just doesn't have that many words.

We're talking about a comic strip style story, one that tells a tale, with different things happening but doesn't have lots of paragraphs, sentences or words.

Depending on your child's abilities, this exercise can be done without any words at all. The important thing is to have a story that works and makes sense.

It's a good idea to have an example of a comic strip to show your child, unless they are familiar with the concept. If they already read comic books or graphic novels, they will know what it should look like. If not, then buy a comic or find one online to show them, so they can see how the pictures tell the story, supported by little snippets of dialogue and description.

Starters

For the first part of this exercise, your child chooses one of the starter ideas below and decides how the story will turn out. They can change whatever they like, or simply follow the steps given, as long as the story is told in a comic book style. Each picture should tell a part of the story in a clear and simple way.

As with earlier exercises, drawing skills aren't as important as the ability to organise events within the story.

Here are some starter ideas, with steps to follow.

The New Shoes

The old shoes are broken

The new shoes shine

They move by themselves

Oh no!

Party Puppies

Ten sweet little puppies

One is very naughty

The dinner is on the table

Where is the dinner?

Water Everywhere!

I hate swimming

I'll hide here

Everyone else is swimming

What does this tap do?

I can't turn it off!

Magical Music

Boring old music lesson

What is that new song?

Where did the teacher go?

Where did the school go?

Twenty lollies

Sweets are great

Lots of money

Sweet shop, here I come

Mine, all mine

A new haircut

I'm not having it cut

You can't make me

I'll be horrible in the hairdressers

I won't sit still

What happened to my hair?

Pet Fish

A present for my birthday

A beautiful fish tank

Big, big fish

Changing colour

What is it now?

Cat food

A greedy cat

Next door has chicken for dinner

Lock the cat in

Where did the cat go?

Where did the chicken go?

Full stories

Children are often more willing to make up their own comic strips because they don't see them as real stories, so they aren't threatened by them.

When you think your child is ready, encourage them to use the comic strip as a guide to write out their own story, in full sentences. All they really have to do is describe what is happening in the comic strip, explaining and expanding what is going on in the pictures.

For instance, if the picture shows a cat stealing a chicken, your child can say something as simple as 'the cat is stealing the chicken'. The idea is to encourage them to expand a little each time, so this sentence might become 'the cat is stealing the chicken so he can eat it himself'.

It's only a little longer but it gives more detail to the original message in the picture. It's a useful way of showing your child how stories are often just descriptions of things which happen or which could happen.

Optional work

Once your child is used to doing their comic strips, try setting them off with only a few words or an idea, rather than steps to follow. There may still be some resistance to doing this exercise, but as long as you keep it all about the story within the pictures, there shouldn't be the same pressure as when writing a normal story.

Describe, describe, describe!

This is a slightly easier section in that your child isn't going to write a full story, so they might feel happier doing this if they are getting a bit tired of the whole story business. Between you and me, this is not as easy as it looks though.

It is all about description. Having to describe things is a very important part of writing stories and is essential in all areas of literacy. Helping your child learn to describe what they **see** (in a picture or around them) is a good starting point for helping them to describe what they **read** in a full book, or **remember** from their own experiences.

Describe a picture

In this chapter, you need a picture. If possible, make it a photograph and a good size so that lots of details can be seen.

If you like, look at my example picture on the next page and use that to practice with. Sometimes, children find it easier to describe an unfamiliar picture than one they know because the unfamiliar one makes them more curious.

Your child should describe the picture as they see it, then be encouraged to use more detail. This is a stage-by-stage process as they may only offer a few words at first and then, with your help, become more confident in picking out the details.

If necessary, start with single words and build up. I have given different examples after the picture, but listed them on a separate page in case you want to use the picture yourself.

Example picture

Example descriptions

Here are some different ways your child can describe the picture. It doesn't matter which kind of description they start with, just use each one as a stepping stone to the next so that the picture is 'explored' as much as possible.

Talk about the picture to stimulate ideas and don't be afraid to ask questions, such as, what is happening, who is in the picture and so on.

1. Children, girl, boy, brother, sister, playing, game, smiling, home, floor, glasses.

2. Brother and sister, playing together. The sister is older than the brother. They are playing with the toy.

3. The girl and the boy are sitting on the floor. They are playing with the toy and are happy. They are both wearing shirts, so it might be cold weather outside. The girl has glasses and she looks older than the boy. They both look like they are having a lot of fun. I think they are at home.

Different descriptions

Do you see how the descriptions all talk about the picture in different ways? Your child can make the simplest statements about a picture, even down to listing the colours in it and they are still describing it.

Also, they might talk to you in detail about the picture, then only use simple words when they write about it. Don't worry if there is more spoken than written description. It is very important to develop descriptive abilities, so I would rather your child talked for a long time about the picture, than be hurried to write about it and miss out on the detail.

Real life descriptions

You can use this technique in other ways too. Opportunities to describe are all around us and can be used to help your child learn new words and methods of expressing themselves.

This time, I want you to help your child describe the world around them. Rather than looking at a picture, which never changes, let them look at something close by, in the real world.

This could be in a very familiar place, like your kitchen, or somewhere like the local park. Or you can try it in a completely new place, the next time you go somewhere.

It can be more difficult for some children to describe the real world, simply because there is so much more detail. They can become 'over-loaded' and feel they will miss something, or not know where to begin.

Help as much as necessary, even taking it in turns to describe the things you see, a bit like the I-Spy game.

As it is real life and not a picture, you have all the added experiences to describe as well as what you see. So you can now talk about sounds, smells and what happens as you look around.

In a busy place, describing can take a lot longer than when you use a picture. If there is a lot going on, concentrate on the most noticeable things. For instance, in a park you might focus on the playground and not take as much notice of a football game or a dog walker.

Example real life description

For my example, I have used a trip to the supermarket. We are sitting in the car park, near the entrance.

1. Cars, people, trolleys, shopping, doors, cash machine, lights, dog tied up.

2. Busy with lots of people. Some trolleys left around. A dog barking outside. A queue for the cash machine.

3. It was very busy today with a lot of people and too many things going on. The car park has cars moving around and the shop doors keep opening and shutting. Sometimes people stop to pet the dog tied up outside but as soon as they move, he barks again.

Talk about it

You can discuss with your child what you want to include or leave out of the description. If they don't feel happy describing so many different things, then focus right in on something smaller, such as the dog in our example, or the swings in the park playground.

Make your child feel like they are in control of what they describe, so they can relax and concentrate. If they feel like there is too much to deal with, they will hurry through it or refuse altogether.

You could even try describing different things and comparing what you have written down. Make it a secret until you have finished. Again, a bit like I-Spy, you can read out your descriptions to each other and then guess what you are talking about and see if there is anything you have missed.

Some children love 'competing' with their parents and will be keen to show you something else you could have included, so be sure to leave out a few details to encourage them to spot what you missed. This is a good way to build their confidence, as well as making them feel they can be good at describing things.

The Interviews

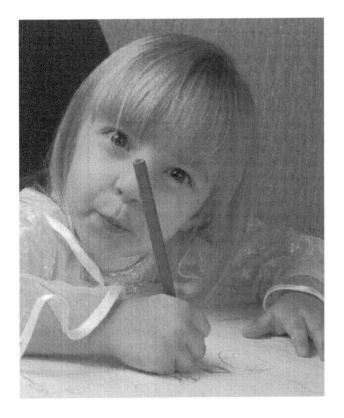

This exercise can work as distraction from the fact that writing needs to be done, though I don't promise anything: children who really dislike creative writing will be able to smell it coming a mile away and will not be fooled!

Your child will be interviewing people they know, friends and family, to build up an idea of how to write down what people say and make it into a complete piece of work. The interviews work in stages, so that the end result comes together naturally. Also, the face-to-face nature of it does take the mind off writing things down, so it can be fun activity for many children.

Ideally, start with someone they know very well. If you like, they can interview you, as a practice run, but as you will help them make up the questions, it is best to start with someone else.

Questions

What to ask? This is where the creative part comes in, as your child needs to think of some questions that can be put to different people. You don't want too many 'safe' questions, or ones which will end up with similar answers from people.

Try to think of a mixture of questions, ranging from basic ones like 'what is your name?' and 'what is your job?' to more expansive ones like 'what did you want to be when you were little?'

For starters, think of ten questions and see if you think they will give good enough answers. You don't want too many that have short and simple answers as that will cut down on the written work at the end.

Example Questions

What is your name?

What did you want to be called instead?

When did you first go swimming?

What is your favourite thing in the whole world?

What would you like to do on your birthday?

Tell me how you would bake a cake.

Can you skip to music?

If you went into space, what would it be like?

How many times have you lost your purse/wallet?

If you were a dog, what kind would you be and why?

The method

If you or your child find this difficult, feel free to use my questions to get you started. You can show your child how it might work by asking them questions and then letting them ask you. This helps you both understand which questions are likely to mean a longer answer.

Do you notice how some of my questions mean asking people to use their imaginations? It's always good to do this as it means your child is interacting with people who are (hopefully) being creative and making it fun.

Make it clear to your child that they should write down the answers people give them. If they have difficulty, help them in this as they can still do plenty of writing later.

Also consider sending the questions by email to people you know who live away. Having the answers written down adds an extra element to the interviews and contrasts with answers written down in the face-to-face interviews.

The writing part

When you have at least two interviews, it is time for the writing practice. You can do many more than two, but try not to gather up too many interviews before embarking on the writing part as it may seem overwhelming.

Your child should already have notes, written down by themselves or a helper. These notes are the basic answers to their questions. What they need to do now is write them up in a slightly different way – and it is only slightly different. We're keeping it simple so they can see the link between the notes they started with and the finished piece of work.

To turn the notes into a full piece of writing, your child needs to add a few extra details. They should describe who the interviewee is and phrase it in a nice, clear way so that readers who don't know the person can imagine them.

Look at how I do it in the example to see how notes can be changed into proper sentences. I haven't written out the full interview, just enough to give you a taste of how it might look.

Example full writing

My Grandma answered these questions on Tuesday night before she went out with her friends. I asked her some questions to find out what she thinks about things.

Grandma says her favourite thing in the whole world is me and her second choice is Mummy. She also said she likes bingo and is going to be late if we don't hurry up.

If she was a dog, she wants to be a great dane because then she would be able to reach everything and would be able to run along the beach.

Extra thoughts

It can be a good idea to warn interviewees to give as much detail as they can. You want to avoid people saying 'I don't know' or not really taking it seriously. The last thing you want to do is have your child feeling bored or being put off because other people won't answer their questions.

It can be a nice idea to decorate the finished interview either with a picture of the person or a photograph of them, so it looks a bit like a magazine article. If you want to take it a step further, the finished work could be written out in neat, or typed and printed and given to the interviewee as a present.

This is a good way to make your child more enthusiastic about doing the work as they know they have a good result in mind, making someone happy by giving them a very personal and individual present.

Before and After

In this chapter, we're going to look at descriptive writing again, but in more depth. Lots of words are descriptive and your child should be getting more used to using them by now. What we are going to do now is help them to write about what they feel, as well as what they see.

Firstly, make your child very happy by saying there is no writing to start with. You need to make some masks, both for you and your child. If this is difficult, or you don't have supplies to make masks, then think of a way to cover your face, without obscuring it completely.

What you should aim for is a way to completely change the way your face looks, so that when your child looks at you and also at their own face, it is almost like looking at a different person.

This can be a little scary for some children and encouragement might be needed. If you think your child might be uneasy, talk about it. Explain it is simply a way of looking at people you know and seeing them in a new light. It won't be for long and it's only to help with the dreaded writing.

Once you have made your masks, set them to one side. It's time to write!

As you are

Descriptive writing can be harder or easier if you know a person. Ask your child to write down what they think when they look at your face. There should be three main sections to this, but let them write more if they can. Try for at least two sentences for each section. Look at the example below for more help here.

As usual, if you need to start in a simple way, talk about it first and perhaps write descriptive words as a list, before putting them into proper sentences.

1. A simple start, asking them to describe what they see when they look at your face.

2. How would they describe you if they didn't know you? This is a way to make them look at you logically, pretending they don't know you. What would they say then?

3. What do they *feel* when they look at you? Try to draw them out from a simple answer such as happy, sad or even bored!

Example As you are

This doesn't have to be a complicated or long piece of writing, but see below how different words can be used to describe thoughts and feelings on a familiar subject.

1. Daddy has brown hair and his nose is fat round the middle. One of his eyebrows is up.

2. He is a man with brown eyes and a hairy chin. He is old enough to be a daddy.

3. I like my Daddy because he's going to make me pancakes for tea. I like to watch his nose move when he's going to sneeze.

And again

Now, do this part of the exercise again, with your child describing themselves. Let them look in a mirror and point out what they can include, if they need help.

Children often find it easier to describe themselves than other people, though you might need to guide you child when it comes to writing it down as proper sentences.

Example And again

1. I have light brown hair and brown eyes. My ears stick out!

2. She is a girl with long hair and a butterfly hair clip. She is smiling.

3. I am feeling happy and I like the way my butterfly sparkles in the mirror.

You see how the description changes when the child talks about themselves? Remind them, for number 2, to talk as if they are someone else.

On number 3, it is not a standard description of feelings, but shows how the child can write about themselves. Be flexible as you go along and don't worry if not every exercise is exactly as it is in the book - this is all about confidence in creative writing, not making children think in the same way as everyone else.

Masks

Now for the masks! You are going to repeat what you have done so far, but describing how you look while you are wearing your masks.

Think about how this might change what you say about a person. What is hidden? What might you notice instead of noses or beards? How much harder does it become to describe a person? Would the mask itself be the focus?

Example masks answers

Look at my example answers. I have given them only for describing the parent, just so that you can see how it might change the responses.

1. Daddy is wearing a big, red mask with splodges of blue on it. His ears stick out at the side and his hair is sticking out at the top.

2. The man is wearing a big red mask and he looks a bit scary. He keeps sneezing behind the mask.

3. I don't like the mask and I wish it was a kitten mask like mine.

You might notice that descriptions written about the mask are more about feelings than what a person looks like. You may also need to talk about these answers more before your child is comfortable writing them down.

Usually, they will either focus entirely on the mask, as it's something new to write about, or single out the more familiar features, such as your hair at the sides. Do try to help them blend the descriptions, so that they include some of your features and some of the mask's.

A Little Note…

Before we start, I admit it, this is a sneaky one. I apologise in advance to the poor child who thinks it's just a game and enjoys the creative writing. Right, guilt out of the way, on we go.

Choose a time when you are at home with your child and don't have to rush off anywhere. You don't have to do anything special, you just need some extra time for this to work properly.

Now, for at least half an hour, you aren't going to speak to each other. No, you haven't fallen out and I'm not going to make you sulk either. Instead of talking, you are going to write notes.

Anything you have to say to each other must be written down. The complicated stuff, the asking for a drink, the wondering if Aunty Bev is coming for tea today - all of it. To make it more interesting, add pictures to decorate the words.

For this one, you can choose different ways to complete the exercise, depending on what you think will make it more fun for your child or their own abilities. Feel free to make it all in pictures if necessary, but there must be something being said by the pictures. Don't just accept a picture of the dog, it should show the dog eating out of the fridge, if that's what your child needs to tell you.

The words can be simple and very basic, or they can be proper sentences. They can start as one and develop into the other. Make your own responses match as much as you can, so it feels like you're playing the game together.

Don't be afraid to tease your child a bit, to make them change the way they respond. For instance, if they are saying simple things like asking what time it is, reply by writing 'none o' clock!'. If they want to tell you off, make them write it down.

Example notes

Here is an example of how it might go but don't rely on it too much as this kind of exercise can be very flexible.

Alice: Pancakes? (picture of pan, middle coloured yellow)

Dad: Already ate them

Alice: Did not? (picture of angry face)

Dad: Full tummy (bad picture of stick man with fat tummy)

Alice: Been here whole time, no pancakes! (even angrier face with red coloured in)

Dad: Make later, feel like a nap (stick man lying on floor)

Alice: I'll make them myself while you sleep (picture of smiley face with brown hair)

Dad: I hid all the pans

Alice: I'm going to eat all your pudding now (picture of smiley face with cake all over it)

Dad: I give in, I'll make pancakes

Alice: With choc sauce?

Dad: I ate the chocolate sauce

Alice: (picture of stick man with stick girl kicking him)

In-depth

You see, it doesn't have to be true or serious, but if you like the notes can be completely based in real life, very simple and with no pictures. It's an exercise in writing on the spot, with no help and very little guidance. By making it a game, the pressure is off and your child is able to write what they like and not feel it's right or wrong.

You can always help things along by getting it wrong yourself. If your child is a good speller, make a few mistakes. If they can't spell, include very bad drawings. If you both use only pictures, see how much action or detail you can include.

Above all, make it about *creative communication*, even if the communication part is only about when it'll be bath time or whether there are any clean socks.

By helping your child to write quickly, without much thought and with zero worrying, you are going to improve their overall attitude to writing and creativity in general. They might not see the link and you don't have to point it out to them - it's one step in a journey that will lead them to more independence and enjoyment of the written word.

My Life

Again using real-life as a basis for story writing, we're going to start with the past and present to create some writing. This sometimes doesn't seem like creative writing, but it is as it means your child is thinking about how to describe something, what they should write about first, what to leave in and take out – all the things you need to do when writing a made up story.

To begin, your child needs three short pieces of writing. They are factual and descriptive, all based on what they know. They don't have to sound like a story. As usual, do let your child use pictures to answer the questions if necessary or to make it more enjoyable.

1. Who I am

Just as it sounds, this one should be all about your child. Let them decide what should be included. Give guidance if it is really needed but try to let them work it out for themselves. If in difficulty, look at the example later in the chapter.

2. Where I am

This is often an easier one. Your child can describe where they live, who they live with, what their school is like. They can describe only their own house or include their town, village or city. Again, let it be up to them.

3. Who I love

This part should be about their loved ones, family, friends, pets, teachers, toys. Anything that matters to them, from a beloved relative to the pony they like to pet on their evening walk. For this one, you should need to give less help but you can suggest people or things they might include, if they get stuck.

Example Ws

I have given short examples here, as everyone is different. I only want you to have an idea of what can be included and how it might be described.

1. Who I am: My name is Alice and I am 10 years old. I have long brown hair and brown eyes and I like cats, lizards and butterflies. I want to be an explorer when I grow up.

2. Where I am: I live in a tall house in the middle of town. I have a tiny back garden and I planted a flowery bush to help the butterflies. My house is really close to the park and the shops.

3. Who I love: I love my dad and he loves me. We have lots of cousins but we only see James and Greta. We all meet up at the park and play games. I love my best friend Molly and we see each other nearly every day.

Switch it

Now you have to help your child change the way they talk about themselves to make it seem more like a story. There are two parts to this. One is that they are going to talk about their future and the other is that they will be talking about themselves in the third person.

This means instead of writing 'I' and 'we' they would write 'she' and 'they'. Your child writes about their own life and experiences but makes it sound like they are talking about someone else.

For this part, it can help to write it normally, about themselves, then change it to sound like someone else. This would mean writing it out twice, which might not be very popular, so decide beforehand which way you think will work best.

I want...

Now your child is going to write about their future and what they would like to happen. Give them freedom to choose whatever they like, even if it makes no sense or is imaginary.

They might have a clear idea already of what they want to happen in the future, or you may need to suggest a few things. Bear in mind, the future can be tomorrow or next week, as well as years from now.

This part of the exercise should be a little more detailed than the earlier ones, so encourage your child to write more. If you like, discuss it first and then help them to write about your conversation.

If necessary, use these phrases to help your child decide what to write about:

When I grow up…

After school at the weekend…

At Molly's party…

In tomorrow's lunch break…

If I win the lottery…

When I get a pony…

When we move house…

After I learn to drive…

If we go to the pet shop…

A year from now…

Example future

Here is an example, using one of the phrases above.

If we go to the pet shop on our way home from school tomorrow, I'm going to ask Dad to buy a kitten. I don't mind if we have a small garden, we can still have a kitten and let it play out when it's nice. I want to have a white cat or a ginger one and I want it to play with me. I'm going to build it a little house from cardboard boxes and teach it tricks. I really want a kitten and soon I'm going to have one!

In-depth

You see how writing about the future brings out hopes and dreams, as well as planning? This can be very useful in stimulating writing practice as it is more exciting that just writing about what you did over the holidays.

This kind of exercise can be repeated using different ideas. You can even use the phrases above and work your way through them, over time. By keeping in mind that your child is writing about themselves and their own ideas and dreams, you make the writing very personal, as well as simpler to work out.

It is always easier to write about yourself and think of what you like to do than thinking of completely new ideas for imaginary characters.

Friend or Foe?

Following on from talking about themselves, your child is now going to make up a new character, using their own personality to help.

For this exercise, we need to start by helping your child work out what kind of person they are. Later, this description will be turned around to make a character who is the opposite of your child.

he description of their personality can also extend into talking about how your child looks. As they will be writing about an 'opposite' person, they might want to create someone who looks like their opposite too.

Ask your child to make a list of words which describe them. Try for at least five, but ten would be better. Here is a list of possible words – use them to guide your child but don't let them just choose from the list. At this stage, they need to think of their own words, if possible.

Words

Happy, sad, naughty, good, kind, clever, smart, loving, fierce, amazing, sleepy, pretty, handsome, quick, greedy, honest, creative, enthusiastic, logical, playful, friendly, funny.

Description

Once there is a good list of words, which shouldn't be too similar, then let your child write a short description of themselves. Include the physical description too. What you are aiming for is a clear description of your child, written in the third person, which could be read by someone who doesn't know them.

Refer back to the previous chapter for how this can work and do feel free to use earlier work if it seems to cover the same ground. This part of the exercise is mainly to help your child make up a new character, so it's not vital for it to be completely new work.

Example words and description

Words chosen were: *funny, kind, naughty, playful, clever*

Description: *Alice is a **kind** girl with lots of friends. She likes to **play** with them. She is sometimes **naughty**, but she doesn't mean to be and is **clever** at getting out of trouble.*

I haven't repeated Alice's physical description from earlier chapters, as this example is just to help you show your child how to make a good, simple description which tells the reader what they need to know.

You see how you don't need to use all the words to make a good description? It can help your child feel happy to have a good list of words, as then they don't feel they might run out of them (and so run out of things to write).

The opposite

Now your child needs to create their new character, who will be the opposite of themselves. It can be a good starting point to look again at the words they chose when describing their own appearance and personality and think what they could use as the opposite words.

Don't be too exact for this; mainly you are looking for them to create a character who would seem very different from them. It's not essential for this new character to be called 'bad' if your child called themselves 'good'. You could call the new character 'naughty' or 'mischievous' for instance.

Once the new words have been chosen, your child can turn them into sentences, describing the new character in their own right. Don't forget they need a name and it can also be useful to say how old they are too.

Example opposite

Gina is 12 and very tall with short blonde hair. Her eyes are green and she has a sharp face. Gina is serious and likes to be by herself. She is sometimes too quiet with people. She likes to play at home and only has one friend at school.

Do you see how different Gina is from Alice? We don't know how tall Alice is, but from earlier chapters we know she has brown hair and eyes. Gina is blonde with green eyes. Alice has lots of friends, Gina likes to be by herself and has only one friend. Alice is playful and funny, Gina is serious and quiet.

Gina is not necessarily a bad person. Although Alice describes herself as kind, she doesn't make Gina unkind or nasty, just quiet and not as sociable. This is important, as someone can be an opposite without being bad if the other is good.

Friends? Foe?

Now they are going to make friends…or are they? For this part of the exercise, your two characters are together. Your child is one character and the made up person is the other.

Talk about this with your child. Will they be friends with their opposite? Or will they be enemies? Will they start as enemies and become friends? What might happen when they meet?

It's a good way to discuss how very different people can end up being friends, as well as how we sometimes meet people who seem like we wouldn't get along with them until we know them better and realise we want to be friends.

For this exercise, your child can decide what is going to happen. I have included some guidelines below, if needed, but see if they can think of a scenario by themselves first.

What you should aim for are a few sentences, describing what the two characters think of each other and having them be together. Ask your child what they might be doing, if they are getting along, whether they might argue or already be best friends.

Use experiences your child has had to help them think of a scenario, such as what they did at the weekend, or in an after school club. Always guide them to take inspiration from real life to help in their story writing.

Scenarios

Going for an ice cream to the beach, disagreeing over what to choose, ice cream ends up being spilled.

Taking turns on the slide then one being bullied by some other children on the playground. What happens next?

Waiting to see the school nurse, keeping each other company or being stuck in the same place without wanting to talk.

Going to the cinema with school and either ending up next to each other (if don't get along) or sitting separately (if friends already).

Working together to find a lost puppy in the park as twilight falls.

Moving next door to each other.

Example scenario

I have kept the example short in case you need to show it to your child. This exercise is very creative compared to some of the others and may be harder for them to do, so by having a short and simple example, you can take off the pressure of them feeling they have to write a lot or make it 'clever'.

Ice cream scenario: *Alice hated peanut ice cream but Gina loved it and bought two. Gina said Alice was being silly and should try to like it. She pushed the ice cream into Alice's hand and Alice dropped it. Gina felt sorry for her and offered her the other ice cream. Alice ate some to please Gina.*

Middles Only

This exercise can work really well for children who hate the story-writing process of a beginning, middle and end. They do get tired of hearing about that and being told how to start a story and how it must make sense. For once, that is being thrown out of the window.

Choosing any subject they like, your child should write only the middle of the story. They can think about what happens at the start and the end, but they shouldn't write that part of the story.

A good way to do it is, once they have decided on the subject of their story, get them to plan it loosely, either by talking or in bullet points. This is just to give them an idea of what happens when, so they can move onto deciding where the middle is.

It can be best to choose a middle area where something is happening, as action is more interesting than description. If you jump in at a point where something is going on, it also makes it more exciting to read and write about.

Let your child decide their own story, if they want to. Otherwise, use one of these starter ideas and let them fill in the details instead.

Starter ideas

Something strange is happening at school. There is a horrible noise coming from the cupboard in the hall. No one has seen the headmaster for three days. Suddenly...

Champion the sheep dog was sick of herding sheep. He wanted to go to the circus and become a clown, but first he had to find out how to walk the tight rope.

Wendy wanted to go on holiday. Her mum said they could go when they had enough money. Wendy started doing a song and dance act in the middle of town, to make money. Then one day...

The geese were everywhere. It felt like they had taken over the world.

Ethan turned on the computer and heard music coming from it. There was no game running and he couldn't make it stop. Even when he turned the volume off, the music still came. Then...

What could she do? As soon as the watch stopped, everything went wrong. It wasn't her fault it broke, but they all thought she was to blame.

Planning

Choosing an idea of their own or one of the above, now ask your child to bullet-point the different parts of the story. This is only to help them plan, so if they are keen to start writing, instead of planning, do let them.

Where will the middle be? How far past the start do you need to go? Try to think of a place you can start that will leave the reader confused as to what is happening, but wanting to know more. The idea is to make the story sound silly, or interesting, or exciting, without giving away exactly what is going on.

Example plan

For this example, I have used the broken watch scenario.

Granny gives watch for birthday

Hannah doesn't like it but pretends to

Goes to school wearing the watch

Watch broken when she comes home

Granny cries and her mother shouts

Brother says she broke it at school

No one believes it broke by itself

Hannah has to promise to help pay for a new one

The man at the shop finds out the watch has a flat battery

Hannah is out of trouble and gets cake for tea

Having a plan can be really useful but it doesn't mean the details have to stay as they are. Once the story is written down, new ideas might spring up or ones already thought of might not work, so let your child know they can change things as they go along.

The middle

Once they have their plan, think about where the middle will be. This is where the real writing begins. Your child will be writing part of a story, mostly based on their own ideas. It can be difficult, but make sure you encourage them to have a go and see what happens. Remind them it is only the middle which needs to be written and not a whole story. If it really doesn't work, let them choose a different scenario.

Example middle

Hannah sat in her bedroom, sulking and kicking her feet on the wall. She didn't care how much more trouble she got into, she would be in trouble whatever she did. Why did they blame her for everything? It wasn't even her fault! How was she meant to know how it happened?

Still frowning, Hannah glared at the door as her brother came in. He grinned and wagged his finger at her.

'Who's been a naughty girl then?' he asked.

She threw a book at him and he ran out, laughing. Hannah hated them ALL!

Make it better!

For this one, choose a very familiar story, preferably an old folk story, like Goldilocks or Jack and the Beanstalk or a simple picture book story that isn't very long.

What your child needs to do, is re-write the story. Not the whole thing, unless they want to, but definitely the ending.

By looking at a familiar story, it can be easier to think of how you might change it, especially if you have sometimes thought it should be different anyway. How many of us have felt sorry for the bears when Goldilocks wolfs down their porridge? Or what about the poor giant, having all his treasures stolen by Jack?

Think of some possible stories before you discuss this exercise with your child, so they have a choice in front of them. It can be useful to read through one or two, to see which one appeals or would be the best for a re-write.

Planning

What is going to be changed? Only the end, or other parts too?

Plan out what can be different. Don't be afraid to help your child with this, as it's more important that they enjoy the exercise than sit and think by themselves.

Can you add anything to make the story better? Could Jack steal more things from the giant? Could there be a longer chase scene, with Jack in more danger before the giant is stopped? Will Jack become a giant?

Write down some ideas, without worrying about using them all. This frees your child up to think of more ideas as there is no pressure to make them all work.

Example planning

I'm using the story of the Three Little Pigs for my examples in this chapter. Here is how your child's planning might look. Be flexible, though. This planning might have a lot more to do with discussion than writing.

The three little pigs wanted to leave home to become wolf hunters

They thought they were very brave and wanted wolf-skin rugs

They built weak looking houses to fool the wolf into coming closer

He missed the first pig when the house fell down on him

He missed the second pig when he accidentally set fire to the wood

The third little pig's house was crowded with all the pigs in there

The wolf wanted to eat them and they wanted their wolf skin rug

All three pigs ran out, screaming, ready to catch the wolf

The wolf ran away, screaming and went home to his mother

The three little pigs never saw him again

Do you see how the familiar story is still present in the changes? They still leave home and build three houses and they still encounter the wolf all the way through. Unlike the original, no one is eaten in this story but your child might like to make things a bit more gory!

The main writing

Now your child can write out the story in their own words. This part doesn't have to be as long as the original. You don't want to spoil their enjoyment of the process, although it is important to write down their main ideas.

This is where your child can decide how many of their changes to include in the finished story. It's likely, if they have enjoyed the exercise, that they have a lot of new ideas but unlikely they will want to spend a long time writing them down in a proper story!

Don't push things but do encourage them to include at least two or three of their ideas into the new version of the story. This way they change enough to make it different without making it too difficult to enjoy.

Example main writing

I'm keeping this example short, so that it's more like one your child would produce, but look at which changes I have decided to use and how they change the story.

The three little pigs couldn't wait to have their new wolf-skin rug. They built traps that looked like houses and watched for the wolf coming. He was cleverer than he looked and escaped the traps. They all ran out at him, screaming, to catch him. The wolf ran away as fast as he could and never went near them again.

This story can be nicely decorated with lots of pictures and can even be presented as their own book if you like. It's a really good opportunity to link up a familiar story with everything your child has learned so far.

The main aim here is to help them think about stories and how they are put together. By adding their own ideas and changing things, they become a part of the story and also find it easier to see how stories are created, rather than being solid creations, which are never changed.

Film and TV

For this final chapter we're going to bring together the nasty stuff like planning, writing, describing, imagining and general creativity and bundle it up into a nice exercise about films and TV.

Like some earlier work, this exercise involves the technical side of writing but helps children ignore this and enjoy themselves instead. The skills used in this section are directly transferable to many school activities and a good basis for all-round creative thinking too.

Favourite film or TV programme

Many children will have written book or TV reviews at school, so the concept of writing about something they have seen or read might not be unfamiliar to them. If they haven't done one before, or have forgotten, simply explain they are going to think about something they really enjoyed watching and write a little bit about it.

Firstly, talk about what your child has enjoyed watching, either as a film or a TV programme. What you want to do is help them choose something they will remember well enough to write about without having to watch it again. If you have the film or programme, they can watch it again but beware of doing this if your child is adept at distracting you from making them do their writing!

Summary

At this stage, it is only a small amount of writing. Once they have chosen something to write about, they need to break down what they say into two main areas:

A summary of what the film or programme was about

A few words about what they felt or thought about it

This is keeping it really simple as it's just a warm-up for the next part of the exercise. Don't be afraid to let them talk about their chosen film or programme in some detail, even if only a few sentences are written down. The most important thing is to get them thinking about it.

Example summary

For this example, I have used the film Wreck-it Ralph.

Wreck-it Ralph is about a video game character who likes to wreck things but has adventures in other games.

I liked this film because it was funny and a lot happened in it.

You see how short the summary can be? It doesn't have to be this short, sometimes it can be more difficult to write a small amount about something we really like. Try to keep the summary to only a few sentences all together though.

Plot

Now it's time to write down the plot of the favourite film or programme. Not in very great detail, just enough so that you can see the beginning, middle and end of the storyline.

This might be more difficult with a TV show as they often have storylines that carry on over a few episodes. If this is the case, either choose a story arc to write about or one episode to focus on.

To minimise stress, do this in a guided way, labelling the beginning, middle and end on a piece of paper and leaving a few lines for each. This means your child can go back and fill in any extra details in the right place, if they forget anything.

This part of the exercise helps to clarify the order of most films and TV programmes, showing how they have an organised structure that can be explained simply.

Example plot

Beginning: Ralph has to wreck things in his video game. He is tired of being the bad guy and wants to try living in other games.

Middle: Ralph finds himself in a girly racing game and makes friends with Glitch, who wants to win a race.

End: Ralph helps Glitch win the race and save her game from the evil racer and scary space bugs. He goes back to his own game and is happy.

Again, the plotline can be quite simple. You might need to help with the order or in deciding where different events belong, as in beginning, middle and end.

Favourite character

Let your child choose one character from the film or TV programme. They should write a few sentences on why they like the character, what kind of person they are and what they do in the story.

If they are unsure how to explain these things, talk about their favourite scene with their character and ask them to write about that first. Thinking of the way a character acts can help your child work out what kind of a person they are.

Look at the examples below for more help.

Example favourite character

Favourite character: My favourite character in Wreck-it Ralph was Glitch because she was naughty and funny but really wanted to be a good racer. She turned out to be the princess in the game.

Favourite scene with character: I liked it when Glitch was learning to drive her new racing car and Ralph had to help her. It was funny to see her driving a car made of sweets, especially when she glitched and made it all go wrong.

The description of the favourite scene can explain what kind of person Glitch is because it is a funny scene. Glitch 'glitches', which is her special talent and gives a clue to her being someone special in the game too.

Do-it-yourself

Now for the big part of the exercise. Your child is going to have a go at thinking of their own film or TV show. For this part of the book, I want them to be as free as possible in their choices, so although I give suggestions and starter questions, do try to let them think of as much as they can by themselves.

Firstly, help them decide if it is to be a film or a TV show. Look at my suggestions below and prompt where necessary. If your child comes up with their own idea quite quickly, then don't divert them by suggesting other things.

Suggestions

Film : action, comedy, animated, horror, adventure, fantasy, science fiction

TV show: as above, or game show, reality, documentary, talent, educational

Once you have an initial idea in motion, then let your child work it out as they go along. They should be writing down some ideas of how the film or programme will turn out. Use the previous sections in this chapter to help.

If possible, encourage your child to think of a name for their film or TV show. This can really help them formulate their ideas and can be easier than trying to think of a name later, when all the ideas are in place.

For instance, start with a summary then work out a basic plotline. It doesn't have to be detailed at all, it's not the same as writing about something you have already watched.

Once they have decided on the story or theme, ask your child to think of a main character to write about. If it is based on a TV show, this could be the host, a contestant and so on.

Look at my examples below for help with this section. As always, do let your child lead the way, especially at this stage of the book.

Example summary, plotline and character.

Summary: Tess in Trouble is about an old dog who finds herself lost in the woods and winter is coming.

Beginning: Tess leaves the family picnic and follows a rabbit trail. She gets lost in the woods.

Middle: Tess is stuck in undergrowth and has to bite her way free. She finds a little wildcat in the woods and it shows her the way to an old cottage. No one is there.

End: Tess smells a very old trail from the cottage to the edge of the woods. She takes the wildcat with her and finds her way out. They both return home and Tess has a new friend to play with.

Favourite character: Tess is brave and clever and kind. She wants to find her way home and loves her little wildcat friend. She rescues them both and keeps the little cat safe.

Like other exercises, this one can be repeated in different ways. Trying other themes or storylines is a really good way for your child to find out what they like writing about and what they find easier to do.

Optional extra

If you and your child are happy with the ideas, suggest they write them down as a small story. It doesn't have to be much more than a re-write of the summary, plotline and so on, or it can be a fully-fledged story in its own right.

This could be something worth trying if your child is very enthusiastic about their idea or you could leave it until they have practiced this section and are more confident. It can feel complex to them, to change one type of writing into another, but is always worth trying as it helps them to see how all writing is flexible.

Optional example

Tess loved going on picnics. She liked to explore where they were and then have her treats.

One day, she explored too far and was lost in the woods. It was cold and dark and she couldn't find her way out.

She got stuck in some undergrowth and was trapped. In the morning, she bit her way through the sharp branches and was free.

Then she saw a little cat looking at her. It was a bit different from the cat next door. It watched her, then walked away and looked back. She followed it.

The little cat led her to an old cottage in the middle of the woods. No one had been there for a long time. Tess sniffed about and found a smell that went back into another part of the woods. She followed the smell and the little cat followed her.

Tess led them both out of the woods and they were found by some people walking their dogs. Tess was taken home and the cat went with her. Tess's family loved the little cat and it loved them.

Tess was very happy to be living back with her family and to have her new friend there too. She never wandered off again.

In the end...

I have helped many children overcome their dislike and fear of creative writing. Most of the time, it is down to bad experiences or a rocky start in their education, rather than any lack of ability.

You notice I use the word fear in my first sentence? That has a lot to do with the attitude of some children as they get older and are more fixed in their belief that they cannot and will not write stories.

They decide, for whatever reason, that literacy and creative writing is not for them and avoid it as much as possible. They become afraid to try as it always seems to go wrong and they often feel like they are in trouble when this happens.

It's no good making them work or telling them off, or even bribing them to try harder. You need to find out the root causes and build up the skills needed to do the work in the first place. Patience is more important than any other attribute now.

So much can be achieved by combining dedicated patience and new approaches. Let your child lead the way, allow them to set the pace of their achievements. Don't let their uncertainty and fear dictate what happens in their creative writing experiences.

And those children who simply detest creative writing? These are really few and far between, but they know who they are. Some children are never, ever going to like it or enjoy it. At best, they will bear it and come away from their work feeling pride as well as relief.

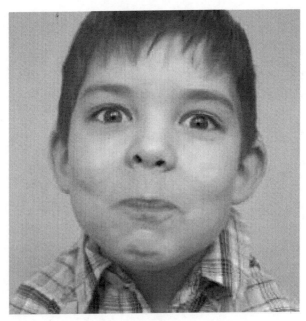

For those children, for the ones who would rather sing Viking ballads in front of the class than write a story, this book should hopefully make it all a little more bearable. I am not promising every child will learn to love the written word, but at least I can make it something they don't mind as much as they did before.

Whichever kind of child you have, remember that creative writing is only creative thinking expressed in a different way. Creative thinking is what will carry your child through life and make problems flexible and situations more fluid. Never forget to remind your child that being able to think creatively is what matters in the end; the ability to write about it is a bonus.

For free resources and news of upcoming titles, please visit

http://freebrians.blogspot.co.uk/

If you enjoyed this book, please consider leaving a review. Thank you!

Printed in Great Britain
by Amazon.co.uk, Ltd.,
Marston Gate.